Gone Fishing

Felice Arena and Phil Kettle

illustrated by
Susy Boyer

First published 2003 by
MACMILLAN EDUCATION AUSTRALIA PTY LTD
627 Chapel Street, South Yarra, Australia 3141

This edition first published in the United States of America
in 2004 by MONDO Publishing.

For information contact:
MONDO Publishing
980 Avenue of the Americas
New York, NY 10018

Visit our web site at http://www.mondopub.com

04 05 06 07 08 09   9 8 7 6 5 4 3 2 1

ISBN 1-59336-359-1 (PB)

Library of Congress Cataloging-in-Publication Data

Arena, Felice, 1968-
    Gone fishing / Felice Arena and Phil Kettle ; illustrated by Susy Boyer.
    p. cm. -- (Boyz rule!)
    Summary: Jamal and Joey go fishing with Joey's father. Includes facts
    about fishing and questions to test the reader's comprehension.
    ISBN: 1-59336-359-1 (pbk.)
    [1. Fishing--Fiction.] I. Kettle, Phil, 1955- II. Boyer, Susy, ill. III. Title.

PZ7.A6825Go 2004
[E]--dc22
                                                            2004045805

Project Management by Limelight Press Pty Ltd
Cover and text design by Lore Foye
Illustrations by Susy Boyer

Printed in Hong Kong

Contents

Jamal   Joey

CHAPTER 1

Before Catching
the Big One

Best friends Joey and Jamal have
gone fishing with Joey's father to a
river not too far from where they live.

While Joey's dad finds the perfect spot to cast out his line, Joey and Jamal wander off and pick a good spot for themselves. Joey tries to place a worm on a hook while Jamal looks closely over his shoulder—it is his first time fishing.

Jamal "Do you think a worm feels pain?"

Joey "No."

Jamal "But it's wriggling a lot."

Joey "Yeah, that's what a worm does, especially when it has a hook stuck in it."

Jamal "So then it is in pain."

Joey "No, it's not. It's a worm. It doesn't feel anything."

Jamal "What about if we use bread as bait? I could use pieces of the sandwich Mom made me."

Joey "No way! Fish like worms. That's what they eat."

Jamal "Well, I might still use bread anyway."

Joey "It doesn't hurt them—really. Cross my heart and hope to die, stick a needle in my eye!"

Jamal "What about a *hook* in your eye?"

Joey "Yeah, good one! Just look at it. It's not in pain."

Joey raises the worm on the hook only inches away from Jamal's face. He then suddenly screams out, "RAH!!!" Jamal jumps back startled, falling over onto the tackle box. Joey laughs.

Joey "Gotcha!"

Jamal "Really funny. I'm still gonna use bread."

Joey "Then you're not gonna catch anything. Here, give me your hook. I'll put a worm on for ya—scaredy cat!"

Jamal "I'm not scared."

Joey "Yes, you are. Just like a girl—
like my sister Sarah. She freaks
out over everything. Even ants."

Jamal "No way! I'm not like that.
Give me a worm then. I'll show ya."

CHAPTER 2

Waiting for the Big One

Jamal puts a worm onto a hook even though he almost feels like throwing up while doing it. Joey is ready to cast his fishing line.

Joey "Okay, fishies, here we come!
Stand back, Jamal, I don't want to
hook you or you'll end up like
Mrs. Hurley."

Jamal "Mrs. Hurley, our teacher
Mrs. Hurley?"

Joey "Yeah. Why do you think she's got a pierced nose?"

Jamal "Because she's really trendy and cool?"

Joey "Nope! 'Cause she got a fishhook caught in it. One of the older kids told me."

Jamal "No way!"

Joey "Yup. She went fishing with
her boyfriend once and stood too
close to him while he was throwing
in his line. The hook got stuck
right in the side of her left nostril.

"When her boyfriend got it out, the hole was so big that she decided to put a diamond stud in it to cover it up. So, you'd better stand back, unless you think you'd look good with a pierced nose."

Joey throws his line in and Jamal does the same. Both boys just sit and wait.

Joey "I think I've got a bite."

Jamal "Really? That's quick!"

Joey "Shhh! You'll scare it away."

Jamal (whispering) "Do you think it's a fish?"

Joey "No, it's a crocodile."

Jamal (whispering) "Really?"

Joey "Duh! Of course it's a fish! But I think it's gone now."

Jamal "You know, I got my highest score last night on 'Beetle Raider 3000'—I got 52,022 points."

Joey "Cool! Is that Level Six?"

Jamal "Yup."

Joey "I can only make it to Level Five. Jamal, look! Quick! You've got a bite and it's a big one."

CHAPTER 3

Catching the Big One (Almost)

Joey and Jamal struggle to reel in a large fish that has hooked itself onto Jamal's line. Suddenly the line goes loose. The fish has got away.

Joey "Oh, man! Did you see that! It was humongous."

Jamal "Unreal! It felt like it weighed a ton."

Joey "That's for sure! I can't believe it got away. I bet it was the biggest fish in this river."

Jamal "How big do you think it was?"

Joey "At least as big as us, even bigger. It would've been a world record in fishing."

Jamal "Aww, cool! I would've been famous. I would've been interviewed on television and everything."

Joey "What do you mean *you* would've been famous? We *both* would've been famous."

Jamal "Yeah, but it was my line."

Joey "So? It was my fishing rod. I'm gonna tell Dad that we almost caught a big one. Just wait here and look after my line. It might come back again."

Joey runs over to his dad, then returns to Jamal.

Jamal "Has y'dad caught any?"

Joey "Nah. He just said he's enjoying the serenity."

Jamal "What's serenity?"

Joey "It sort of means peaceful, I think."

Jamal "You mean like being bored?"

Joey "Yeah, sort of. Are you bored?"

Jamal "Yeah, a little. And hungry!"

Joey "Then have that sandwich your mom made."

Jamal "I can't. I just gave it to a whole bunch of fish."

Joey "*What*!?"

CHAPTER 4

Forgetting the Big One

Joey looks down at the water and is amazed to see a large school of fish swimming near the surface gulping and nipping at the sandwich Jamal has just thrown in.

Joey "Great idea, Jamal! Look at
'em all! I'm gonna try to catch one."
Jamal "Me too!"

Both boys scramble for their
fishing rods, scaring the fish away in
the process. Disappointed yet again,
they sit down waiting for them to
reappear.

Joey "That was amazing. There
must've been twenty of them."
Jamal "Yeah. I wish they'd come
back. It'd be a shame to waste
what's left of the sandwich."

Joey and Jamal wait patiently without saying a word to each other, for what seems a very, very, long minute.

Joey "Have you played the new game called 'Fishnet?'"

Jamal "No. Is it any good?"

Joey "Yeah, it's awesome. You have to net as many fish as you can in a set time to get to the next level. It's in the car. You wanna play?"

Jamal "Yeah, let's go!"

Joey and Jamal make their way
back to Joey's dad's car. Joey's father
calls out to them. "What about the
fishing?"

Joey and Jamal (chuckling) "That's what we're gonna do."

A few minutes later Joey's father joins Jamal and Joey in the car, ready to take them home.

"So, Jamal, what did you learn from your first time fishing?" he asks before driving off.

Jamal looks up, while Joey continues to play his game.

Jamal "Um...fish really do like bread, and bring a game just in case you feel a little serenity creeping in."

Jamal

BOYZ RULE!
Fishing Lingo

Joey

bait What you put on your hook so that you might catch a fish.

fishing rod What you use to catch a fish. The fishing line attaches to the end of it.

freshwater Water that doesn't have salt in it. Most rivers are freshwater.

sinker A small metal ball you tie onto your fishing line to keep the line under the water.

snag When you get your line caught on something under the water.

BOYZ RULE!

Fishing Musts

☞ Make sure you have bait on the hook before you cast your line into the water. If you don't want to catch a fish, don't put any bait on your hook!

☞ If you are looking for worms to use as bait, look in the garden. But when you are digging, make sure that you don't dig up any plants.

☞ Make sure that you throw back any undersized fish that you catch.

☞ Only keep as many fish as you think you can eat.

☞ When you cast your line don't cast too close to trees or you might get your line tangled in the branches.

☞ To catch freshwater fish, you should fish in rivers, lakes, or ponds.

☞ If you go fly-fishing, you don't have to put live flies on your hook. Fly-fishing flies are handmade and not real.

☞ If you are fishing from a boat, make sure that you wear a life jacket.

☞ Remember to take some money with you when you go fishing. You might need the money to buy some fish at the fish shop on the way home.

☞ When you find a really good fishing spot, make sure you don't tell anyone. You don't want all the good fish caught before you go back there!

Fishing Instant Info

The most ferocious freshwater fish is the South American piranha. It has razor-sharp teeth. The piranha loves blood and the taste of flesh. In 1981 more than 300 people were killed and eaten by piranha when their boat sank in Brazil.

The biggest man-eating fish is the great white shark. The average length of a great white shark is between 12 and 16 feet (3.7 to 4.9 meters).

The largest mouth in the world belongs to the bowhead whale—it can be up to 16 feet long, 12 feet high, and 8 feet wide (4.9 x 3.7 x 2.4 meters). Its tongue weighs about one ton (900 kilograms).

The longest animal in the sea is a type of jellyfish called the Arctic lion's mane. It can grow up to 150 feet (46 meters) long.

The largest sea-living mammal is the blue whale. Its average length is a massive 80 feet (25 meters). Some blue whales have weighed as much as 190 tons!

The least experienced fisher-kid always seems to catch the most fish.

The worse your line tangles, the more fish seem to have been caught by everyone else.

The largest fish ever caught was a 59-foot (18-meter) whale shark. It was captured in 1919, in the Gulf of Thailand.

Think Tank

1 What do Jamal and Joey use for bait?

2 What does Jamal say he learned from his first time fishing?

3 What do you use a sinker for?

4 Why shouldn't you move around too much or make too much noise while fishing?

5 Where can you go to find worms for bait?

6 What should you do if you catch an undersized fish? Why?

7 What should you always wear when you are in a boat? Why?

8 When you are fishing from a boat, is it better to go alone or with a friend? Why?

Answers

8 It's better to fish with a friend because it's safer.

7 You should always wear a life jacket when in a boat in case you fall out or the boat capsizes. It will help you keep afloat.

6 You should throw undersized fish back in the water so they can grow up and reproduce.

5 You can dig in the garden for worms. You can also buy worms in a fishing shop.

4 Because you might scare away the fish.

3 A sinker keeps your hook underwater, where the fish are.

2 Jamal says he learned that fish like bread, and to bring a game in case you get bored.

1 They use worms as bait, and also bread.

How did you score?

- If you got most of the answers correct, you must be an expert fisher.

- If you got more than half of the answers correct, then maybe you need to get some fishing lessons.

- If you got less than half of the answers correct, you'd better get your fish from a fish shop.

Felice → ← Phil

Hi Guys!

We have lots of fun reading and want you to, too. We both believe that being a good reader is really important and so cool.

Try out our suggestions to help you have fun as you read.

At school, why don't you use "Gone Fishing" as a play and you and your friends can be the actors. Set the scene for your play. Try not to get the line caught in anyone's hair. Maybe you can use your imagination to pretend that you are about to catch the biggest fish ever.

So...have you decided who is going to be Joey and who is going to be Jamal? Now, with your friends, read and act out our story in front of the class.

We have a lot of fun when we go to schools and read our stories. After we finish, the kids all clap really loudly. When you've finished your play your classmates will do the same. Just remember to look out the window—there might be a talent scout from a television station watching you!

Reading at home is really important and a lot of fun as well.

Take our books home and get someone in your family to read them with you. Maybe they can take on a part in the story.

Remember, reading is a whole lot of fun.

So, as the frog in the local pond would say, Read-it!

And remember, Boyz Rule!

Felice

BOYZ RULE!
When
We Were Kids

Phil

Felice "What's the biggest fish you ever caught?"

Phil "I once caught a fish that was so big it needed a tow truck to take it out of the river."

Felice "So what did you do with it?"

Phil "I threw it back because it smiled at me so I felt sorry for it."

Felice "Was anyone there to see this giant fish?"

Phil "No, I was by myself."

Felice "Sounds fishy to me!"

BOYZ RULE!
What a Laugh!

Q What's a good name for a man who likes fishing?

A Rod.